CHIMERA SKIES: BEN

SHARLENE HEALY

CONTENTS

1. Chapter 1 1

2. Chapter 2 5

3. Chapter 3 8

4. Chapter 4 13

5. Chapter 5 16

6. Chapter 6 21

7. Chapter 7 25

8. Chapter 8 29

9. Chapter 9 31

10. Chapter 10 36

11. Chapter 11 40

12. Chapter 12 43

13. Chapter 13 46

14. Chapter 14 50

15. Chapter 15 56

16. Chapter 16 59

17. Excerpt of Secret Skies   62

About Author   64

Also By   65

CHAPTER ONE

T HE TRUCK BOUNCED UP as I hit a bump in the road. A grunt of pain came from the seat next to me and I glanced at Pearl. Her eyes were closed but tears streamed out of her eyes as she adjusted her arms.

"You okay?" I asked.

Pearl groaned. "What do you think? Just get to the bunker."

I'd only known Pearl a couple of months now, but I never heard her snap like that before. She must be in incredible pain. I gripped the steering wheel and pressed down on the pedal, not caring about the speed limit. Technically, I shouldn't be driving without an adult since I only had my learner's permit, but who cares. Pearl needed help. The next time I saw Mom, I'd have to tell her that sneaking out to drive with friends was preparing me for the future.

A glance at the rearview mirror showed that Rita and her family were still following me. They hadn't left yet. Pearl coughed and I looked over to make sure she was okay. Her face was paler than it was a minute ago. Clenching my jaw, I looked back to the road and revved up again. I was going about ten miles above the speed limit, and I'd have to keep my eye out for any cops.

At the start of our drive, Pearl had told me that she could get us into Bunker 3. Our plan was to drop her off at Bunker 3, and I'd leave and go back to my family. I wanted to help them find our parents. The closer we got to our turn-off, though, the more sure I was that we would need to get her help at a real hospital.

I drove, my eyes steady on the road as the trees rushed by. Pearl kept her eyes closed but she coughed every couple of minutes so I knew she wasn't asleep. Medicine wasn't my thing, but I figured it wouldn't be good if she fell asleep.

I heard a faint noise and looked at Pearl. She had her eyes open and was watching the road, too. "Turn off onto that dirt road," she said, pointing her chin toward a turn-off.

I gripped the steering wheel again and my heartbeat accelerated. She did not look good. I turned off the road and drove until the road ended. I parked the car on the side of the road, the tires kicking dirt up all over the truck. Oh well; it wasn't ours anyway. I yanked my door open and jumped out. Rita and her family had stopped behind me, but no one was getting out. I glared at them as I ran to the passenger's door. I didn't have time to babysit. Pearl wasn't going to be able to walk; I knew that just from one look. I'd have to carry her. I slid one arm under her knees and one behind her back and pulled her across the seat until I was cradling her. The entire time, I had my jaw clenched. I needed to go slow so I didn't hurt her more but time was running out. I stepped away from the truck, holding Pearl close, and glanced at Rita. They had the doors open but weren't following.

"If you want to come then hurry," I said, turning to Pearl. "Where to now?"

"Straight," she said, her voice faint.

Ugh. I held her tight and headed straight, hoping that I wouldn't jostle her too much. The trees surrounded us and I walked straight, but I wasn't sure how long I was supposed to. "Pearl," I said. "How long do I go straight?"

She didn't answer. "Pearl," I said, trying again.

Pearl opened her eyes. "At least half a mile."

I glanced behind. Rita and her family were following. I rushed forward, heading deeper into the forest. Pearl kept her eyes open at least. I swear, I was checking on her every five seconds. It wasn't long before her eyes were closed again. "Pearl," I said. "You have to stay awake."

She opened her eyes and stared at me. "Okay."

I clenched my jaw. I pulled Pearl closer so I could check my watch. We'd been walking for about five minutes. I pulled my arm back, giving Pearl more room, and she didn't even make a peep. Great, her eyes were closed again.

"Pearl," I said. "I need to know where to go."

She didn't respond. I tried again, and she opened her eyes to slits before closing them again. The third time she didn't even do that much. I looked up. There were trees all around; no way was I going to be able to find that tree entrance by myself. Pearl needed help now and I wasn't going to waste my time searching for one tree in the forest, either. I gritted my teeth and turned around.

"Rita. You and your family camp here. I need to take her to the hospital," I said.

"No," Rita said. "We're staying with you."

My eyebrows drew together and I pushed my lower jaw out over my top teeth. "I can't wait for you."

"We'll keep up," Rita said. "That guy said stick with you. We're going nowhere."

I grumbled and pushed past them, stalking off as fast as I could without hurting Pearl. Even when I wasn't around him, Max was a pain in my butt. Since it was a straight walk to the truck, I had no problem retracing my steps. I was good at directions, except when it came to looking for bunker entrances in the middle of nowhere.

The truck door was still open so I stepped up and leaned against the seat, Pearl in my arms. At least she was still breathing, even if it was shallow. I shut the door with a little push, and ran to my side to hop into the drivers seat. I revved up the car and the tires kicked up more dirt as I swung the truck around like the doughnuts my friends and I did in the highschool parking lot last year. Once I was facing toward the road again, I stomped on the gas pedal and sped away.

I kept one hand on the steering wheel and used my other hand to pull out my phone and turn it on. It was charged, thankfully. I missed my little pocket friend. I pulled up my *Maps* app and searched for the nearest hospital. To my surprise, more than one popped up. So many of the cities nearby were small and I expected there to be maybe one hospital in the entire area. I hit the closest one, which was still about twenty minutes away, and the directions popped up.

The speed limit sign glared at me as I drove by. It was just a suggestion, right? I looked at Pearl, her shallow breathing uneven, and decided it was definitely just a suggestion. I hit the gas pedal again, going double the speed limit. Despite the slowdowns and turns, it took ten minutes to get to the hospital. I sped right up to the emergency room entrance and threw open my door. Once again, I slid my arms around Pearl, trying to keep her steady as I picked her up out of the truck. I whispered into her ear, "Everything's going to be okay. I'm not going to let you die."

I ran through the automatic doors and rushed to the desk.

"She needs help now," I said to the woman sitting at the desk. She took one look at Pearl—covered in blood, pale, hardly breathing—and pushed a button on the desk that called for help over the PA system. A man dressed in scrubs wheeled a bed over. He and another worker took Pearl from me and strapped her to the bed. They wheeled her off and I tried to follow, but the lady at the desk stopped me with a clipboard.

"Stop right there," she said. "You need to fill these out."

My shoulders dropping, I took the clipboard and sat down in one of the waiting room chairs.

Chapter Two

FIVE HOURS. I'D BEEN in this waiting room for five hours. During those five hours, I asked the desk woman—who told me to stop calling her "hey you" a million times—when I could see Pearl. I couldn't even concentrate long enough to finish more than one episode of my favorite anime I'd turned on in an attempt to distract myself. I paced. I sat down. I stood looking out the window, but nothing helped me calm down. I still had no idea what was going on with Pearl. I didn't know where she was, what was happening, whether she was alive or dead. No one would tell me anything because I wasn't family. If I had known, I would have told them she was my sister so I could get some answers. I rubbed my head and looked out the window again. Rita was standing there, leaning against a tree. Oops. I'd forgotten about them.

I walked outside, but not before the desk woman asked me to hurry and fill out the paperwork again. I grunted and ignored her. Rita was still propped up against a tree, and I walked up to her. "You guys can go. Get a hotel or something. It's going to be a while still ," I said.

Rita looked at me. "You're a little young. Do you need help?"

"No," I said. "Go find food or something."

I turned around and headed back into the hospital. "We'll be back soon," Rita said, her words following me as I walked away.

"Hey you," I said to the desk woman. "Can I see her again?"

"I told you, stop calling me that."

I stared at her.

"No. She's in surgery now."

"Fine," I said. "Do you at least have any extra phone chargers?"

She sighed and pulled open a drawer on her side. "Have a look."

I leaned over and saw a ton of cords and plugs. I reached in and grabbed the one I needed. "Wow, there are a lot."

"People leave a lot. Fill out that paperwork."

I ignored her and went to sit down near a plug. If Pearl was in surgery, who knows how long I'd be here, but at least she wasn't dead. There's no point in operating on a dead person. I dragged another chair close and propped my feet on it. This way, it was easier to slouch in the chair until I was comfortable. The best part: I could prop up both elbows on the chair armrests and hold my phone right in front of my face. I watched a few episodes before a man in scrubs sat down next to me. He started talking before I'd paused and I turned to him and said, "What was that?"

He grunted and started again. "You're the one that brought the girl in? How old is she? What happened?"

I sat up in my seat and put my phone down under my leg. There wasn't much I could honestly tell him. "She's seventeen. We were attacked by a bear when we were hiking," I said.

"Are you her brother?"

"No," I said. "She's my friend."

"What's her name?"

"Pearl," I said. I couldn't remember her last name.

"Pearl what?"

I shrugged and didn't answer.

He sighed. "You don't know the last name of your friend?"

I lifted my shoulders again and didn't respond. He put his paper on his lap and rubbed his forehead. "Look, kid. Can you at least call her parents?"

"I'll try," I said, lying through my smile.

He stood up and turned to leave but I pulled on his sleeve. He looked down at me with eyebrows drawn together. "Wait. Is she alive?" I asked.

"Yeah, kid. She's alive. Barely."

He walked past the front desk through the double doors. When I couldn't see him anymore, I slumped down in my seat. No doubt there would be more questions.

A couple hours later, I finally got some more information out of the desk lady. Pearl was transferring to the ICU and would have to stay the night. She wouldn't tell me what was wrong or what room they were moving her to. She glared at me when I handed her the blank paperwork. I grinned at her and left. Night was coming and I needed to figure out where to sleep.

Rita and her family were sitting at a table with Melly running up and down the sidewalk. I walked up to them and let them know what was going on. I tried to get them to go hide in the forest again, or at least get a motel, but they refused. Oh well. It wasn't my problem what they did.

As for me, I planned to park in the lot and sleep in the truck. I didn't want to stray too far from Pearl. Also, I didn't have more than fifty dollars on my card. I'd be able to go see Pearl in the ICU tomorrow right away if I was closer, too.

CHAPTER THREE

S UNLIGHT PEEKED OVER SOME clouds and I groaned as I sat up.
My neck cracked when I moved it side to side and I could feel a kink
in my torso. If I were a foot smaller, sleeping in the truck wouldn't have
been so bad. It would have been better if the truck didn't smell like a gym,
either. I grabbed my charger and stuffed it into my pocket. Outside, I
stood on the gravel and twisted my back to try and stretch out the kink.
Stretching didn't get rid of it completely, but I didn't care. Today I was
going to see Pearl.

I walked into the hospital and headed toward the elevator. The floors
were labeled with their departments and I hit the button for ICU. When
the doors opened I walked through and headed straight in. There was a
short hallway that led to a giant desk with a line of computers on it. A
bunch of people wearing scrubs were sitting down, talking, and joking.

"Hey," I said. "A girl was transferred from the ER. Can I see her? Her
name is Pearl."

A male nurse with a stethoscope around his neck twirled his chair until
he faced me. "Are you related?"

I clenched my jaw and then relaxed it again. He was just asking. "No.
I'm her friend."

"Okay. Our visiting hours are from nine to five, then. Come back in two hours."

A quick glance at my watch told me that he was right. It was only seven in the morning. I'd have to waste two hours before I could see Pearl.

"Is there anywhere to get food?" I asked.

"There's a cafeteria on the first floor. Follow the signs," he said, turning his chair back to his colleagues.

***

The cafeteria had a wide selection of choices. I ended up getting a couple of pizza slices and some orange juice before I found a table to sit at. I picked a table that was right next to a wall charger and I plugged my phone in. Since I was out of Bunker 3, I wanted to see if there were any news articles or posts about chimeras. I typed it into a search engine and page after page mentioned the mythological creature chimera. There was a linked video of an episode of *Full Metal Alchemist*. I had some time so I rewatched it before going back to my search. It took a couple of pages, but on page seven of the search, there was a forum on some webpage dedicated to conspiracies. The post was titled "Strange monsters kidnapped my neighbors," and I read the whole thing.

The descriptions of the monsters sounded exactly like meras. There were hundreds of comments of people who thought they'd seen one, too. Some could definitely have been ruled out as delusional, but they couldn't all be fake. I bookmarked the webpage to come back to later and packed up my trash. It was nine now, and I'd be able to go see Pearl.

The hospital wasn't too busy, and there were only a handful of people on the elevator with me. The only experiences I'd had with hospitals were from movies and TV shows. I wasn't one to voluntarily walk into a place like this. Still, at least this one was clean and nice enough. There was only one nurse at the station when I arrived and she directed me to the right room. I walked in and paused, my breath caught in my throat while my heart banged against my ribs.

Pearl was on a bed with all sorts of tubes and monitors hooked up to her. There was a cuff wrapped around her arm, a bunch of wires coming out of the top of her hospital gown, and one tube going in her nose. She also had tubes coming out of her arm and her finger was in one of those things they measure oxygen with. I couldn't remember the name. She was asleep, even with the monitors beeping steadily. I took a deep breath and walked in, dragging the chair next to her bed.

For the next few hours, I sat next to Pearl while she slept. Nurses and staff came in and out, checking her monitors, replacing the bags hanging on a metal pole attached to the bed, and cleaning the room. The nurses were friendly enough, but they never had time to stop or tell me why she needed surgery and how long she'd be there. They always told me they'd talk about it with her parents later.

Right before lunchtime, a woman wearing a black blazer and jeans came into the room. She carried a storage clipboard. Her tag said case manager, whatever that was.

"Hello there!" she said. "My name is Maggie. I'll be your caseworker. Do you have your insurance card?"

I stared at her. "Uh. I don't."

She flipped through her paper and jotted something down. "Hmm that's okay, we just need it before you leave. What's Pearl's address? And her parents' phone number?"

"Uh. I don't know."

Maggie squinted her eyes at me, looking back and forth between me and Pearl. "Do you know where her parents are?"

I didn't say anything to that. I mean, I knew where her mom was in a general sense, but that wasn't going to help here.

"Okay. Do you know where your parents are?" she asked.

"Yep," I said, keeping my face as neutral as possible. "They're camping in the woods."

"Okay," she said, her eyebrows drawing together. "Can you get a hold of them? Your friend is pretty badly injured."

"I guess I can call them," I said.

"How old are you?"

"I'm sixteen," I said, drawing out the word. I didn't see any harm in telling her.

"Sixteen?" she looked concerned. "Look at your friend. She's seriously injured. Do her parents even know she's here? That's something they need to know."

"Yep," I said.

She sighed and clipped her pen to her clipboard. "I'm going to have to make some calls."

She left the room with a huff, clearly frustrated. I started pacing the room. There was no way I could keep answering the questions the hospital needed. Pearl should have her mom with her anyway. Taking a deep breath, I sat down and put my hand into Pearl's and said, "It's all going to be okay. I'm going to figure this out."

I felt the tiniest squeeze. It gave me hope. I whipped out my phone and typed as fast as I could. I searched for Bunker 3 but nothing came up. I searched for Jane Summers but a ton of results popped up. I scrolled through countless social media profiles until I found the one I was looking for. The picture was of Ms. Jane on a beach with an adorable little puppy. Of all things, the leader of a secret underground bunker had a social media profile. It was going to save me, though. I clicked on the profile and sighed in relief when messaging was available. I opened the app and typed in *Ms. Jane. It's Ben. Look, Pearl's in the hospital. It's pretty bad. She needs her mom.* I held my breath, my heart racing as I watched the app. My message was marked delivered, and a few seconds later read. Then three little dots popped up. Thank goodness. *We'll be there soon.* Where? I sent her the location and room number and the three dots appeared again. *30 min.*

I sent back a thumbs-up emoji and sat back, slouching down in my chair again. Holy crap. They were on their way.

Chapter Four

IF I HAD THIRTY minutes before they got here I wanted to grab some food now. I didn't want to be away when they arrived.

The cafeteria was more crowded than it was earlier and I had to stand in line to order my pizza. I could never get sick of pizza. The workers packaged it up for me in a Styrofoam container so I could eat in Pearl's room. I grabbed a root beer on the way out and headed back up to Pearl's room.

When I got there, her bed was raised and her eyes were open. I set my pizza down and rushed to her side.

"How are you?" I said. "They wouldn't tell me anything."

She grimaced and said, "I feel great until I move. My nurse has me on pain meds, but they don't always work."

I squeezed her hand. "We can get something stronger."

I coughed and shuffled from foot to foot. "Um. There's something you should know," I said.

Pearl stared at me until I continued. "Ms. Jane and your mom are on their way. The hospital kept asking all these questions I couldn't answer."

Pearl tilted her head up and winced before looking back at me. "You know Ms. Jane will take us back to Bunker 3. You can't go back to your family."

I shrugged. "Guess you're stuck with me."

"Poor me," said Pearl with a wink.

Now that I'd confessed, I sat down in the chair and started eating my pepperoni pizza. Pearl watched, stabbing me with her glare.

"What?" I said with a mouthful. "You can't have pizza?"

"I'm literally going to punch you in the face."

I grinned. "I'll buy you some before we go back to Bunker 3. My treat."

"You'd better," said Pearl, closing her eyes and relaxing into her pillow.

By the time I finished my food and thrown away the trash, Pearl was sound asleep. She'd been sleeping a lot, but I guess it was understandable since she'd had surgery and was now recovering. There was nothing left to do now but wait for Ms. Jane's arrival. It was nice of Pearl to think about me not being able to rejoin Sam; I knew what was important, though. Likely the hospital would have called the police. Then we'd never see anyone. I didn't want to go back to Bunker 3. Norman was there, and he wasn't our biggest fans. Or maybe he was our biggest fans and that's why he was intent on using us for his experiments.

I wanted to be out there, helping my family. But if Pearl's life was more important than staying away from Bunker 3. Tom knew enough to survive. It's not like Sam couldn't take care of herself, either.

A nurse walked in and I watched as she adjusted the machine that had tubes running through it. "She said she hurts when she moves," I said.

The nurse turned to me. "She's on pain medication."

"She said it hurts," I said, my jaw clenching while I glared at her.

The nurse's eyes widened. "I'll see what else the doctor has for her."

Thinking about my family wasn't going to do me any good right now. I pulled up my phone and started scrolling around. I responded to a few social media posts and then went through a few videos of random people. The clock said I only had ten minutes before Ms. Jane arrived. I drummed my fingers on the armrest of the chair. A few more videos kept me distracted until those ten minutes finally ticked by. Ms. Jane and Jewel, Pearl's mom, walked in, right on time.

CHAPTER FIVE

M S. JANE SURVEYED THE room before her eyes landed on Pearl. She heaved a sigh and walked right out. Jewel rushed to Pearl's side and pushed her hair back, murmuring to her the whole time.

"What happened?" asked Jewel.

I was about to tell her when Ms. Jane walked in. "Not right now," she said.

Jewel and I both nodded. Minutes later, a doctor wearing a white coat walked in, accompanied by a nurse.

"Your daughter came to the ER yesterday, carried by this young fellow as I understand it. Both shoulders were injured, and surgery was required. She has metal plates and screws in both scapulae."

The nurse handed him an X-ray picture, which he held up to the lightbox on the wall and pointed while he talked. "She has a broken ankle —which is in a cast now—and mild internal bleeding. She can go home in a few days, but she'll need physical therapy for a few months."

The doctor turned to me, eyeing my dirt and blood-covered clothes, and said, "What happened?"

"Bear attack," I said, my face neutral.

He huffed and turned to Jewel and Ms. Jane. "Anything else?"

Ms. Jane looked down her nose at him. "That will be all."

He turned around and left in a hurry, the nurse scurrying after him. I turned to Ms. Jane.

"A case manager came earlier. She wanted insurance."

"I'll take care of it," said Ms. Jane. She walked to the door and shut it. She turned to me and said, "Now, what really happened."

I looked between Ms. Jane and Jewel, a grimace on my face. They weren't going to like this no matter how much I sugar-coated it. I decided to not even bother and I told them the whole story, except for June's weird device.

Tears leaked out of Jewel's eyes when I told them how the mera crushed Pearl's shoulders. Ms. Jane's face remained impassive throughout the whole story.

"You expect me to believe that the lot of you—eight teenagers with no real fighting experience—took down two meras?"

I shrugged, lifting my hands up. "Believe what you like. The bodies are probably still there. Rita's in the parking lot somewhere, too."

Ms. Jane sighed. "They'll have to come with us. We'll get a hotel for three days until Pearl can leave."

Ms. Jane left again and I leaned forward and put my head in my hands. It wouldn't be long now until I was stuck in Bunker 3 with no internet. Stupid security excuses. Ms. Jane just didn't want to pay for it. Jewel glanced at me.

"Thanks," she said.

"For what?"

"For taking Pearl to the hospital," said Jewel. "We don't have the right equipment in Bunker 3 to help her. She wouldn't have made it."

I shrugged and pulled out my phone to watch some more videos. "No probs. She'll be happy to see you."

Someone brought in another chair for Jewel and we sat in silence, me watching my videos and Jewel reading a book on the history of titanium. Ms. Jane eventually came back in and announced that she had found a place to stay. Then she asked me to introduce her to Rita. I stood up and slipped my phone back into my pocket. I squeezed Pearl's hand and told her I'd be back, even though she was still asleep, before I left.

It didn't take long to find Rita and her family. They were sitting at a table eating lunch and Melly was running around their table in circles. I walked over to them and said, "This is Ms. Jane. She'll take care of you."

I left them to their business and went back to Pearl's room. Rita and her family weren't my problem anymore, as if they ever were in the first place. Up in Pearl's room, Jewel was still sitting on the chair. She had her book in her hand but every few minutes she would glance and stare at Pearl. I sat down and leaned over to Pearl.

"Ms. Jane's taking care of Rita. I know you'd care," I said. I pulled out my phone and caught up on more of my shows. In the middle of an episode, I glanced up to see Jewel analyzing me instead of reading her book. I raised an eyebrow at her before returning to my show. For the next hour, we continued like this until a knock on the door jamb interrupted our quiet. I looked up and it was the case manager, Maggie, accompanied by another woman wearing a skirt and a jacket. She was carrying a clipboard like Maggie.

"Good," said Maggie, "you're still here. We need you to go over what happened again for this nice lady here."

I looked the "nice lady" up and down and turned to Maggie. "No. Byyee."

I brought my phone back up to my face and ignored them both. My phone was low enough to see Jewel over the edge. She looked at me then turned to the two other women. "What's going on here?" she said.

"Oh, hi," said Maggie. "I'm Maggie, this girl's case manager. This is Tina, she's with Child Protective Services."

"Uh-huh," said Jewel.

"And who are you?" asked Maggie, her syrupy sweet voice grating on my ears.

"I'm 'this girl's' mother."

"Oh, perfect," she said. "We have some paperwork for insurance for you to fill out."

"You can leave it on the table and get it later," Jewel said.

I coughed to cover my snicker. Jewel sounded annoyed. I turned to see Maggie shuffling back and forth. "Okay," she said. "But you still need to talk to Tina. Are you aware your daughter was camping alone without a guardian?"

"I'm her mother. Of course I was aware," said Jewel.

"Well, you know, it could be dangerous for them to be unchaperoned."

"But is it illegal?"

"No?" she said. "I don't think so?"

"It's not. I don't see the problem."

"But we still need to know what happened," said Maggie, Tina nodding her head so hard that her ponytail swung back and forth.

"I believe Ben already told you that. It should be in the charts already."

My phone was paused on my lap now as I watched them go back and forth. At this point, Maggie's face was a little red and her eyebrows were drawn together. Tina was grimacing and put her hand on Maggie's arm. Maggie glared at me and threw the stack of papers on the counter. She and Tina made a quick exit and I turned to Jewel, my mouth hanging open.

She shrugged. "What? I'm no fool."

I grinned and was about to turn my phone back on when Pearl opened her eyes and grinned.

"Nice, Mom," she said.

"Pearl!" Jewel said, jumping up from her chair and leaning in close to Pearl. She hovered over her but didn't touch her. "You're awake. Thank goodness. I've been so worried."

"Mom, I'm okay. You can hug me," Pearl said with a little laugh.

Jewel gave Pearl a soft hug and I scooted my chair closer to Pearl's bed. She turned to me and I smiled at her, my face lighting up. I was so glad she was okay. Seeing her in the forest, bleeding, unsure if she was going to live or die. It was horrifying. Exhausting. I'm glad it was over. Pearl winked at me. "Come closer, Ben," she said.

My eyebrows drew together and I leaned closer. I wondered what she wanted. She reached her hand out as if to pat me on the head but before I could blink, she flicked me on the forehead. I jumped back and rubbed my forehead as she chuckled and settled back into bed.

"Seriously?" I said. "Pearl, come on!"

She chuckled some more and said, "Sorry, not sorry."

I snorted then grinned at her before slouching in my chair and returning to my videos.

CHAPTER SIX

T HAT NIGHT, JEWEL STAYED at the hospital with Pearl. Since I wasn't related, the nurses kicked me out and told me to come back tomorrow. Ms. Jane and I walked outside and I took a deep breath, glad I was no longer breathing in the rubbing alcohol smell of the hospital anymore. Ms. Jane looked around the parking lot and said, "What did you use to drive here?"

I pointed to the far end of the parking lot where the truck was still parked. "We picked that up from the city."

Ms. Jane pursed her lips and sighed. "All right. We'll take my car and head over to Bunker 3."

She started walking toward a Jeep but I didn't follow. I sat down on one of the stone benches outside the hospital. When Ms. Jane noticed that I wasn't following her, she turned around and walked back to me.

"Aren't you coming?"

"No," I said. "I'm staying until Pearl leaves."

Ms. Jane stared at me. "No. You're coming with me."

I crossed my arms and stared back. After a minute staring contest—during which I didn't blink once—Ms. Jane sighed and sat down next to me.

"You know it's safer in the bunker, right?" she said.

I shrugged. "Yeah. But she needs me. And I need to see that she's okay."

Ms. Jane rubbed the sides of her head. "The hotel I found had two beds. One was going to be for Jewel. But since she's staying here tonight you can use it. As soon as Pearl's out of the hospital, both of you are coming back to Bunker 3."

"I know."

***

The hotel wasn't too bad. Definitely not the Ritz, but not a dump in the middle of nowhere either. I took a step to plop down on the bed right next to the door, but Ms. Jane stuck her arm out and stopped me.

"You need a shower first. You're covered in blood."

I looked down at my clothes and grimaced. She was right. My clothes were a mess. I was surprised no one at the hospital had made any weird comments about it. I sighed. "My bag is in the truck at the hospital."

Ms. Jane rolled her eyes and muttered something about teenage boys. "I'll go get them. You wait here. Don't sit on the beds."

She turned and left, closing the door with a sharp snap. I sat down on the bed closest to me and bounced up and down a little. They seemed comfy at least. Not wanting to push my luck too much, I stood up and brushed off the spot I'd sat in. Then I dragged a chair in front of the TV and flipped through the stations. I wasn't really in the mood to watch anything. It was bothering me a little, knowing that Pearl was in the hospital and I wasn't there. I wanted to make sure she was okay and that they were giving her the medicine she needed. Of course, I didn't know anything about what she needed in the first place, but they weren't even taking care of her pain when I was there. At least I could help with that. Instead, I was stuck here in a hotel.

I kicked my shoes off and propped my feet up on the entertainment center, settling down into a comfortable position. I flipped through the channels, searching for something interesting to watch, when a picture on a news channel caught my eye. The picture was of the city where we'd found Rita. They were memorializing the "nuclear tragedy" that happened a month ago. The news reporter was interviewing a nuclear scientist and they were debating the need for more regulation to prevent similar accidents. I grimaced. What a bunch of bullcrap.

I left the channel running in the background and took out my phone to find the conspiracy website from earlier. I spent the next hour searching for theories on the nuclear tragedy to see what people thought. It wasn't surprising that most of them were wrong. The most voted on theory was that the nuclear tragedy was to get rid of the evidence of the lizard people that ran the government. That made me chuckle. Although, when you considered that meras were the ones running the government, lizard people weren't that far off.

I was still reading the theories when Ms. Jane opened the door. I looked up and she was carrying my bag from the truck and a takeout bag. She took one look at the bed and said, "You sat on it, didn't you."

I looked at her and blinked. How did she know? I said, "No, you said not to."

"Uh-huh," she said. She threw my bag at me and said, "Go shower and change. I brought food."

Inside the shower, I held up my dirty clothes, unsure what to do with them. It's not like I was going to wear them again and I definitely wasn't cleaning them. I shrugged and threw them in the corner behind the door. Good enough.

After my shower, I stepped out of the bathroom while rubbing my head with a towel. Ms. Jane was on her tablet, typing away with one hand while one hand was twirling chopsticks. The food containers were neatly lined up on the table. I filled up a plate and sat down. Ms. Jane didn't even glance up at me as I ate, so I took out my own phone and read more conspiracy theories. When I was finished with my food, I left my plate on the table and hopped into my bed.

"Hey," said Ms. Jane. I looked over at her and she pointedly looked at my plate. I sighed and got out of bed to throw away my plate, then returned to bed. She said thanks and continued to work on her tablet. It was already 11 P.M. and even though I was used to staying up later than this, last night I slept horribly crammed into that truck. I plugged in my phone and wrapped the blankets around me until only my face was exposed. I closed my eyes and said, "Night."

"Night," said Ms. Jane. "We'll go see Pearl nice and early. Get some rest."

I grunted and buried myself into bed even more and went to sleep.

Chapter Seven

T HE SOUND OF A running shower woke me up and I pulled the blankets over my head and groaned. My watch informed me that it was six in the morning, which was way too early for any human.

The next thing I knew, Ms. Jane was shaking my shoulder, so light that at first I didn't notice. I pulled the blankets down and looked at her with groggy eyes.

"What?" I said.

"It's 7 A.M. Let's go get food."

"You know they don't let visitors in before nine, right?" I said.

Ms. Jane grinned. "After all you've done so far, you're going to let that stop you?"

My mouth dropped open and I threw the covers back and bounded out of bed. I never expected Ms. Jane would encourage me to break some rules, but I'd take it. Today was the third day that Pearl was in the hospital, and I was hoping she was feeling a lot better. When I was ready to go, Ms. Jane and I walked to her car. I hopped in and she started it up, backing out of the parking lot slower than even my mom does. I drummed my fingers on the side of the car the entire way there. Ms. Jane went exactly the speed limit. Not a tick less, not a tick more. Sure, I guess it would create problems for a whole ton of people if she were in trouble with the police, but seriously? She could have at least gone five miles over. I sighed and settled my head on the chair.

We arrived at the hospital and headed straight to the cafeteria. Ms. Jane looked around then said, "Get whatever you want. I'm buying."

Score. I grabbed a few slices of pizza and a giant orange juice and met her at the checkout line. She had a tray with an egg omelet, a cup of fruit, and chocolate milk. Dang it, I didn't know they had chocolate milk. Oh well. As promised, Ms. Jane paid for the food, even though she raised an eyebrow at my selections. We sat down at a table and ate in silence. After we finished, Ms. Jane piled the trash on her tray and told me to go dump it since she paid. Sighing, I threw the trash away. I brushed my hands off and Ms. Jane and I started walking toward Pearl's unit.

"Now, the key is to walk straight to her room like you belong there," she said. "Don't hesitate, and be confident."

I nodded and squared my shoulders, trying to look confident. Ms. Jane laughed as she watched me. "Just walk normally," she said.

We arrived at the ICU and walked straight to Pearl's room. One nurse half stood as if to stop us, but Ms. Jane stared at her and she sat right back down. I grinned as we walked into Pearl's room.

As soon as Jewel saw us she said, "Perfect, you guys are here. I need to get food, but I don't want to leave Pearl."

"Mom," said Pearl, "I told you I'm fine."

Jewel leaned over and kissed Pearl on the forehead. "I'll believe it when you're not in a hospital bed."

Ms. Jane and Jewel started talking to each other at the door and I sat in the chair closest to Pearl's bed.

"Hey you," I said, grinning. I noticed she didn't have the tube in her nose anymore.

"Hey you back," she said.

"I was thinking, do you need a handicap now when we play games? You know, since your shoulders are all messed up."

"Honestly, even with my shoulders like this, you're the one that'll need a handicap to keep up with my scores."

I shrugged. "It's no big deal if you can't handle it. I'm not judging."

"I will literally throw my controller in your face," she said, with a huge smile.

I grinned back at her. "No more nose tube?"

She groaned, her happy smile still lingering. "Nope, they took it out earlier this morning. They're transferring me to another unit today."

"So you can go home soon?"

She nodded. "Yep. Also, did you eat pizza again? I can smell it on your breath."

I shrugged. "Ms. Jane was buying. She never said I had to eat anything specific."

Pearl laughed. "You're so weird."

I made a face at her and she laughed even more. Not wanting to just sit there, I took out my phone and showed her some of my favorite shows. It distracted us both until the nurse came to move Pearl to her new room. Ms. Jane stayed to let Jewel know where we were going, but I followed Pearl as the nurse wheeled the entire bed out of the room. The nurse tried to be careful, but Pearl still winced when the bed went over the door bumps on the ground. I handed her my precious phone, hoping that she'd be able to take her mind off the pain.

"Did you miss your phone while we were—uh," said Pearl, eyeing the nurse. "—camping."

"You know it. No internet in the middle of nowhere sucks," I said, drawing out the word "sucks" to make my point. Pearl grinned up at me and returned to watching the show. The new room wasn't as large as the last one, but it at least had a comfortable chair, which I sat in immediately. Ms. Jane and Jewel eventually joined us and said that Pearl would be getting out of the hospital in a few days.

***

The next few days continued with more of the same. Ms. Jane and I would eat breakfast before heading over to visit with Pearl and Jewel. We'd hang out until the staff kicked us out of the hospital and Jewel would stay with Pearl overnight, and Ms. Jane and I would head back to the hotel. Each day, Pearl looked more and more animated. She had fewer and fewer tubes and wires connected to her until finally only one was left on the day she was supposed to leave.

The nurse came and talked to Pearl and Jewel—mostly Jewel—and handed Jewel a giant stack of papers. Pearl had medicines that she'd have to take, so we were going to swing by the pharmacy before we went back to Bunker 3. Ms. Jane said she'd have someone take care of getting the next doses. Pearl would also have physical therapy in Bunker 3 because they had a few physical therapists there already. Her cast would come off in Bunker 3, too.

I was glad we were finally leaving the hospital, but I couldn't face the anxiety building up inside me. Pearl would be taking her time healing. However, I would be alone, with nothing stopping Norman from finding me.

They wouldn't let Pearl walk out of the hospital, so Ms. Jane and I drove to the pickup area. "You ready to go back?" asked Ms. Jane.

"I'm going to miss the internet," I said. "Can't you get it down there?"

Ms. Jane laughed. "If it wouldn't send a signal to the meras that someone was there, sure."

My shoulders dropped, but right then I saw Pearl being wheeled outside the hospital. I hopped out of the car and went to help her. I tried to hold her arm, but Pearl smacked me.

"I can walk, you know," she said.

"Yep," I said. "Like you've never been on legs before."

Pearl rolled her eyes and accepted my help when I offered again. We didn't have crutches for her to use yet anyway. Once we were all loaded in the car, Ms. Jane drove off and headed toward Bunker 3.

CHAPTER EIGHT

M S. JANE DROVE THE car to an abandoned lot about twenty minutes from the hospital. She pulled her car right next to a whole slew of broken-down cars. After we'd all gotten out, she had me help her throw a giant dirty sheet over her car and pin it down under the tires. I slung my bag over my shoulder and stuffed as many of Pearl's things into my bag that would fit. Pearl took careful and slow steps, wincing every now and then. I helped her as much as I could, short of carrying her. Thankfully, it wasn't long until we were in the middle of the forest, around where the tree should be.

Ms. Jane walked up to one of the trees and traced a symbol, the same one Max had. Nothing on the tree looked different; I had no idea how they knew which one led to Bunker 3. Ms. Jane finished and the panel opened, revealing the passageway. I sighed. Here we go again. Pearl heard and looked up at me.

"Don't worry, we'll have plenty to do," she said.

"Yay. Old movies I never wanted to see in the first place," I said, grinning down at her.

"You could read?" she said.

I gagged. "Ew. Read?"

Pearl patted my arm, a grin on her bruised face, and we walked down the stairs to Bunker 3.

***

After walking Pearl to her room, I found my old room and opened it. The room was exactly as we had left it. Nothing changed, nothing moved. Tom's bed was even still wrinkled in the spot he'd sat in before we left. I plopped down on my bed and sighed, staring at the ceiling. Entering the bunker this time had been different since we'd gone through the whole process before. Ms. Jane did inform me that I'd have to meet with her later tomorrow to discuss my "contract." At least she forgot to take my phone. I held it up high and of course, there was no service at all. I tucked it into my bag and stared at the ceiling, a grimace on my face. Tomorrow, I'd have to start up work again. Jewel said she'd be in and out to check on Pearl, but we'd be able to test some new weapons she'd been designing. I turned to my side but then all I was staring at was Tom's empty bed. I should have been out there with them, fighting to find our parents. Instead, there I was, stuck in Bunker 3.

Turning to my back again, I sighed. There hadn't been a choice. If I wanted Pearl to live, she needed to go to a hospital. I closed my eyes and drifted in and out of sleep.

CHAPTER NINE

I WOKE UP BRIGHT and early the next morning. Just kidding, I didn't wake up until noon. I'd forgotten to set my alarm and it's not like I wanted to go to work anyway. I stumbled out of bed and showered then headed to the cafeteria to get some food. It was too late for breakfast, but I was able to get some lunch in me. I took my time eating when all of a sudden I remembered my meeting with Ms. Jane. She wanted me in her office at 1 P.M. sharp, and it was already 1 P.M. I jumped up and threw my trash into the bin before heading to her office.

I looked at the door and frowned. This was not how I wanted to spend my time. I knocked on the door and Norman opened it. Great. The guy who tried to kidnap us for experiments.

"Ms. Jane wanted to see me," I said, not even bothering to hide the disgust in my voice.

Norman opened the door wider and Ms. Jane caught sight of me. "Oh, good, Ben. You're here. Come in. You can go, Norman."

Norman left, making sure to bump me slightly as I walked in. What a tool. Ms. Jane motioned to sit down in the chair across from her and I did so, walking as slow as I could while shuffling my feet. Ms. Jane just stared at me until I was seated.

"Let's get straight to the point," she said. "You broke your contract."

"Huh?" I said.

"The contract. You signed it when you first came here."

"Uh. What did it say again?"

Ms. Jane sighed and pulled a sheet of paper out of a folder. I looked closer and the tab said "Weeks, Ben" on it. She handed me the paper and I glanced at it.

"Oh, yeah, I did sign this."

Ms. Jane rubbed her temples. "Yes. You did. You broke it by leaving Bunker 3 without my direct orders."

"I mean, Norman was trying to kill me. Doesn't that violate the contract?"

"Norman's a different circumstance. Also, he's being punished for his little stunt," she said.

"Yeah, right."

Ms. Jane rubbed her temples again. "The fact of the matter is that you violated the contract and now you'll have to deal with the consequences."

"I'm stuck here with no internet. What could be worse?"

Ms. Jane took a deep breath a few times before answering. "You have two options. Every Friday, you will either work with the Sanitation Department or the Library."

"That doesn't sound so bad," I said. "It says a punishment could be death."

Ms. Jane started to laugh but turned it into a cough and she covered her mouth. "Yes, it's not death. You'll talk to the heads of each department and they'll give you their tasks. You'll also need to keep track of your hours and they'll sign a sheet for me at the end."

I refrained from rolling my eyes. It almost broke my eye muscles, but I did it. It sounded like I was being babysat. "Sounds good."

Ms. Jane sat back in her chair. "You can leave. Bring me or Norman your paper on Friday."

That was only two days away. Great. "Sure," I said. I walked out of the room and ran right into Norman.

"Glad you're back," he said.

"Sure you are," I said, my eyes narrowing as I stared at him. He grinned and sat down in one of the chairs across from Ms. Jane's desk. I shrugged and left. If he wanted the door closed he could do it himself.

I headed toward Pearl's room. Jewel said she'd be resting for the next few days before starting physical therapy. Pearl was excused from work until she was all better. Lucky her. I arrived at her room and knocked. Jewel opened the door and smiled when she saw me. "Ben, come in," she said.

Their room was a family suite, made especially for parents with children. It was two rooms: one small bedroom and a slightly bigger bedroom. The small bedroom had one bed that took up most of the room, but it was big enough for two people. The slightly bigger bedroom was just like the one I was in, but it had a set of bunk beds on one wall with a twin opposite of it. The three beds total were large enough to fit Jewel and her daughters. The room with the bunk beds had flowers painted on the walls and a giant sun on the ceiling.

Pearl was laying on the bottom bunk, propped up by a ton of pillows. She had a book open in her lap and was flipping through the pages. I walked up to her and sat down on the ground next to her. She didn't even look at me, so I poked her in the arm. Not too hard, though; I didn't want to jostle her shoulders too much.

She narrowed her eyes at me and then smiled. "What's up?"

"I got in trouble with Ms. Jane," I said, my grin turning into a frown. "I have to either clean or work in the library on Fridays."

Pearl grinned. "Aww, poor Ben has to work around books."

I groaned and dropped my head against the bedpost. "You have no idea. This is going to be so boring."

Pearl laughed. "Don't worry, we can play video games after you're done on Friday. Something to look forward to."

I perked up. "Good idea. Don't worry, I can still give you that handicap."

She bopped me on the head with her book. "I will win no matter what."

I grinned and rubbed my head. "We'll see."

We spent the rest of the time talking and joking, and she told me about her physical therapy routine that she had started that morning. Her shoulders still hurt, but the pain meds she was taking helped. After an hour, I got up to leave and Pearl reached out and grabbed my hand.

"Ben, I'm sorry."

"For what?"

She looked down, a frown on her face. "If it wasn't for me, you'd be with your family right now."

I squeezed her hand. "Nah, don't be sorry for that. We kicked some mera butt—as Tom would say—and lived."

Pearl tilted her head up at me, doubt still in her eyes. I squeezed her hand again and said, "You're alive. No regrets."

I gently dropped her hand and walked out of the room. Jewel followed me out and when we were in the hall, pulled on my shirt so I would stop walking.

"Huh?" I said.

"You missed work today. Be there tomorrow. We've got some new projects to work on."

"Sweet," I said. "I'll be there. Except Fridays."

Jewel nodded and went back inside. I turned back around to go to my room. The hallways were as crowded as ever as people finished work and went home. I walked straight through the flow of traffic, not bothering to move aside for people. If they didn't want to get hit then they'd move. It worked, too, until I ran right into Norman. I stopped right before we collided and stared at him. I was taller than Norman, so I stared down my nose at him.

"Excuse you," he said.

I swept my arm to the side. "Excuse you."

Norman hesitated before walking to the side of me. He started moving, but when he was right next to me he turned. "You know, if you need to use the BANEP machine again, I can help. You could be stronger, you know. Strong enough to save people. People like Pearl."

I didn't answer and he shrugged before continuing. Gritting my teeth, I continued back to my room. I threw myself on the bed and punched the pillow. I didn't want to admit it, but Norman's words struck me. If I were stronger, I would have been able to stop the mera from hurting Pearl so much. She wouldn't have metal plates in her shoulders or a cast on her ankle. The image of her bloody, pale, and barely able to stay awake wouldn't leave my mind.

I yelled into my pillow for a second then rolled over and pulled out my phone. It didn't have internet, but I had access to the downloaded shows, until they expired that is. I watched a few before giving up and going to bed.

Chapter Ten

THE NEXT FEW WEEKS settled into a routine. I'd get up for work and Jewel and I would work on various projects throughout the day. Then on Friday I'd go to the library or see what the Sanitation Department wanted. The librarians put me to work scrubbing the floors, shelving books, and repairing broken ones. The cleaning people were the same; I spent my time scrubbing floors and toilets and walls. The jobs no one else wanted to do. It was boring, tedious work. I dreaded every Friday and the only thing that kept me going those days was the game nights with Pearl.

Her shoulders were getting better, and now she could move them like normal. The pain was a lot better, too. She didn't need a handicap in the games we played, but I never stopped teasing her about needing one because why not? It was weird, being alone this long. I was so used to having my family around all the time, every day. Especially when we took vacations and were forced to spend all day together.

I hadn't seen those two prisoners that attacked us the night we left, but I saw plenty of Norman. If I didn't know any better, I'd say he was stalking me. He was always somewhere, watching me. It was creepy.

***

In the middle of a workday, I stormed out of the armory into the hallway. Jewel and I had been working on a new type of weapon, but it wasn't coming together as we'd hoped. The other workers in the armory had no idea what we were doing and gave up helping last week. Jewel and I still had hope, though. I leaned my back against the wall and slumped down, putting my head in my hands. I sat there for a few minutes when I saw someone's feet right in front of me. I jerked my head up and saw Norman standing straight above me. I scrambled to stand and folded my arms across my chest.

"What do you want," I said.

"Just to talk," said Norman, raising both hands, palms facing me.

"I'm not in the mood to talk," I said, gritting my teeth.

Norman shrugged. "Okay. I was just going to say that there's another way. I can use BANEP to help you help yourself."

I narrowed my eyes at him and he shrugged again. "I'm in room five. I'll be there the rest of the day if you change your mind."

He walked off, leaving me staring after him.

***

The day did not get any better. I stalked off toward my room, not even taking the time to go check in on Pearl. I didn't want to see or talk to anyone. It was so frustrating, day after day, failing at this weapon. What we were trying to do? It was just too foreign. No one had any examples that we could use to copy. I paced the floor between mine and Tom's bed. The problem was that I didn't know enough about robotics or chemistry. If I was an expert in those fields, for sure I'd be able to figure out our new weapon.

I clenched my fists. No books held the answers. No one knew how to help us. I didn't have time to get three PhD's to make this thing. There were no options left. I'd have to use the BANEP. Before I could think about it anymore, I left my room and headed straight for Norman's room. I took a deep breath and knocked on his door. He cracked it open and smiled at me. It was an innocent smile that only put me more on edge.

"Oh, Ben," he said. "How can I help?"

"You know what you can do."

Norman nodded, then opened his door and slipped out. "Come on," he said. "Let's get the machine going."

Since it was nighttime, there were very few people walking through the halls. Norman didn't pay attention to them at all and said, "What do you want to learn with the BANEP?"

I looked around and thankfully no one was paying attention to us. "Isn't it supposed to be a secret?"

Norman laughed. "The worst kept secret. You didn't answer me. What are you learning?"

I sighed. It was useless to try and be private. I didn't want the entire bunker to know what I was doing but Norman wasn't getting that. "Chemistry and robotics."

Norman nodded. "Those are huge fields. You're going to have to pull up at least three good memories. Start thinking of them now."

We arrived at the hallway where the BANEP machine was. Norman opened a panel in the wall and it slid open, revealing the room. We walked inside and he started turning on the computers. After that, he gave me the vomiting medicine. When I was done, he injected that green chemical in me—I forgot the name—and I sat down at the machine.

Norman stood there, narrowing his eyes slightly at me as if he were studying me. "Okay. You should be good. I'll be back to check on you in a bit."

I nodded and watched as the screen in front of me started playing my chosen memory. For the next hour, I watched as one of my happiest memories played on the screen. I'd chosen the one where I did my first timed run of *Sonic the Hedgehog*. It was one of my proudest moments. I'd just finished watching my memory when the machine beeped. It beeped one more time before Norman came into the room. He took a look at the monitor.

"Wow, done already?" he said. He typed a few things into the computer. "You can take that stuff off."

He helped me take all the straps off and I dragged myself out of the chair. I held onto the edge of the chair and took a deep breath before attempting to walk out of the room. Norman followed me.

"You know, you can use the machine again. You only need a day of rest in between."

I was so out of it that it made complete sense to me. "That sounds good," I said as I stumbled out of the room. Norman grabbed my arm before I fell over and we walked this way until we arrived at my room. I walked in and Norman stared at me, smiling slightly at me as I closed the door.

Chapter Eleven

T HE NEXT MORNING, I woke up only slightly sick. Sam told us that she was really sick after she used the BANEP machine, but I only had a slight headache. I shrugged and made my way to work, hoping that I would be able to figure out some of the intricacies of our project.

That night, after an uneventful workday, I grabbed dinner for myself and Pearl and headed to her room. All of Pearl's family was gone, leaving her sitting on the bottom bed still propped up with a ton of pillows.

"Hey you," she said. "Where were you yesterday? I wanted to talk to you."

I grimaced. "It was tough at work so I went home to rest."

Pearl nodded. "I know, my mom told me your project isn't working."

"Nope."

"Want to talk about it?" she said.

"Nah. I brought you food. Let's eat."

Pearl lit up when she saw that I had brought her favorite snacks— barbeque-flavored chips, and chocolate milk—from the kiosk, as well as a real dinner from the cafeteria line. I showed her the downloaded shows on my phone and we picked one to watch while we ate.

When Jewel and Emerald came back, I packed up and left, waving bye to everyone. I didn't want to interrupt their family time, and to be honest it reminded me that I had none here. I headed toward my room and right before I finished unlocking my door, Norman appeared right beside me.

"Hey," he said. I jumped, not understanding how he got to me so fast. I hadn't even seen him in the hallway when I was walking home.

"Hey," I said.

"Ready for another round?" he said.

"I'm not sure it's a good idea," I said, shuffling my feet and looking down.

"Hmm," he said. I looked up and Norman was smiling a little.

"What?"

"It's just surprising, that's all."

"What's surprising?"

Norman shrugged. "How easily you give up. Aren't you a little embarrassed?

"Not really."

Norman flashed a condescending smile. "You know I was there for that fight. Prisoner 72 got you good. Your sister did better than you. A girl."

"Haven't you heard? Girls can do anything." I turned to my door and started turning the key to unlock it.

Norman nodded. "Of course, of course. But you can't do anything."

I froze, my hand still on the door knob.

"That can change, though, if you want," he said. "The BANEP can teach you anything."

"Anything?" I said.

"Anything," he said, looking at me earnestly. "If you knew mixed martial arts—just an example off the top of my head—you could have gotten out of that neck hold."

I squinted my eyes at him. "Really?"

He nodded. "Truth."

Turning my key the other way, I locked my door and turned to face Norman. "Okay, let's go try it then."

Norman led me back to the BANEP room and we went through the same process as yesterday. We were going to learn mixed martial arts and judo tonight. This time, the memory I chose was the first time I ever picked up a "Gameboy" and played *Pokémon Red*. I had found them at a used video game store and I stayed up all night playing that game. Even though there were newer games out, *Pokémon Red* was still a classic.

The machine beeped and I started to peel the gloves and helmet off. I stood up and right as I took my first step away from the chair, I collapsed to the ground. I dropped my head to the cold tile, not moving for a second. Slowly, I moved onto my hands and knees. It was too much to do anything else, so I stayed like that for a minute. I was still in that position when Norman walked in. He rushed over to the computer and typed for a minute before walking over to me. He held out his hand and pulled me up until I was standing. He kept an arm around my back, propping me up, and walked me that way to my room. I opened it up and right before I stepped in Norman stopped me.

"Rest all day tomorrow. At night you'll feel good enough to use BANEP again."

"I don't know. I feel really weird."

Norman nodded. "Right now you do. Tomorrow you'll be fine."

He walked away, not waiting for an answer, and I locked my door and collapsed into bed.

Chapter Twelve

I WOKE UP, GROANING as I tried to sit up in bed. My head was killing me. It felt as if someone was gripping my head and trying to squeeze my brain out. I stumbled to the bathroom and looked in the mirror. My face still looked the same and my eyes were still brown. A cough racked my body, and blood splattered onto the sink. I felt something warm dripping through my nose and I looked up at the mirror again. Blood dripped down my nose. I grabbed some toilet paper and cleaned up my face. No way was I cleaning anything today. I left the bathroom and went right back to bed.

***

A few hours later, I woke up and felt a lot better. I got ready for the day and walked to the library. It was Friday, and it was the librarians' turn to use me for grunt work for my community service. The main librarian saw me walk in and sniffed. "You're late," she said.

I shrugged. "Sick."

She sniffed again and told me the tasks for the day. I got to work, moving slower than usual. Every time the librarian walked past me, she made sure to sniff. I glared at her behind the shelves and worked slower.

When the day was over the librarian signed my sheet with a grimace. She made sure to cross out the "12" under hours and write in "six". I rolled my eyes as I stuffed it in my pocket and left to go to Pearl's.

Pearl was out of bed, sitting on a chair at the desk at the end of the bed. She had her cast off and was wearing a brace now. "Hey!" she said. "What's up?"

I plopped on the edge of the bed and said, "Nothing. You?"

She held up her notebook. "Just getting some stuff done. Want to go play games in the Game Room?"

I grinned. "Handicap?"

She smacked me on the head with her notebook, laughing the entire time. We headed to the Game Room, talking about random things on the way. We settled in for a game of *Halo*, split-screen style. When we were done, I walked her to her room and headed home.

I was almost to my room when I saw Norman up ahead, walking toward me. He told me yesterday that I'd be fine using the BANEP again, but I didn't want to. Unfortunately, there was nowhere to run, and I clenched my fists as he caught up to me.

"Ready for another round?" he asked.

"No, not today," I said.

Zeek appeared behind Norman. "You agreed to another round. Let's go," Norman said.

I looked from Norman to Zeek. "Nah, I'm good."

Both of them walked closer to me, hedging me closer to the wall. "Let's go," he said again.

Zeek grinned at me, a grin that clearly said *I can't wait to stab you in your sleep*. I narrowed my eyes at them again and said, "No."

Norman looked at Zeek and nodded. Zeek flew towards me and gripped both my arms. He turned me around and started marching me towards the BANEP room. At first, I struggled, but Zeek's grip was strong and I was tired. I gave up and let Zeek escort me towards the BANEP room.

Norman readied the machine and I barely lifted a finger to help. "You're learning jiu-jitsu, krav maga, and yoga."

"Yoga?" I said.

"For flexibility, obviously," said Zeek.

I snorted and sank against the chair. Norman told me I was ready to go and they left the room as the monitor in front of me started playing.

I watched out of the corner of my eye, making sure they didn't see what was on my screen. They could make me sit down, take the medicine, do all this. But they couldn't make me use only happy memories. In defiance, I brought up the memory of our fight with the meras. The memory that still haunted me of watching Pearl get crushed by a five hundred pound monster. I watched as Tom took beating after beating while I stood there frozen.

The entire memory replayed on screen until I stopped thinking at all. As soon as the machine beeped, I ripped off the gloves and threw them to the floor. I stumbled toward the door, fell to the ground, and threw up all over the floor. Groaning, I stood upright as Norman and Zeek walked in. Norman stepped in the vomit on the floor before realizing what it was. "Ew!" he said, stepping backward and shaking his shoe. Zeek simply laughed.

"Oops," I said, shrugging. I dragged myself out of there and headed home as fast as I could, which admittedly wasn't that fast.

Chapter Thirteen

Today was saturday, and there was no need for me to get up early. No work, nothing to get to. I threw my blankets over my head and went back to sleep. I swear I'd only been asleep for a couple of minutes when I heard a knock at my door. Groaning, I swung my legs over the side of the bed and dragged myself to the door. I opened it and saw Pearl standing there with a smile on her face.

"It's Saturday, and you know what that means," she said.

I shook my head. "No. What does it mean?"

She held up the *Halo 3* game case. "Tournament day."

I grinned. "All right. Let's get going."

We left right away and headed to the Game Room. Pearl suggested we grab some snacks before we got started, so we grabbed as much as we could carry. When we got to the Game Room, it was already packed. All the players from our last tournament were scattered throughout the room, waiting for me and Pearl to post the tournament bracket. Pearl started drawing out the bracket on a whiteboard someone had dragged in. We were playing classic red versus blue. One of our regulars had brought in another Xbox 360 and I set up a system link between the two consoles. We were going to play on teams of four. I wished Tom was still here; he was surprisingly good at playing shooters. We'd just have to make do. Pearl made a list of teams, and of course, we were on the same team together.

Our team wasn't playing the first few rounds, so I sat and watched the others play. Eventually, it was our turn and I focused on the screen. Usually, when I play games, I can focus pretty well but I'm always aware of my teammates and what they're doing. This time, for some reason, I could not bring myself away from my own player. There was something inside of me, something that pushed and demanded that I win at all costs. I took out two of their players and before I knew it I had shot one of my teammates.

"What the heck Ben!" said my teammate. "I thought we said no friendly fire!"

I turned and stared at him and he scooted away from me. I shrugged and turned back to the game. I needed to win. A coldness settled over my shoulders as Pearl took out another of their teammates and I took out the last one. Our teammates started celebrating their victory and while they were distracted I shot them both. I would be the last one standing.

Pearl smacked me on the shoulder. "Ben, we already won. What are you doing?"

I looked at her and rubbed my shoulder. "Uh. I—uh. I have no idea. I had to be the last one standing."

Pearl squinted at me, her eyes filled with concern. "Are you okay?"

Abruptly, I stood up. "Yeah. I'll be back."

I left the Game Room as the next teams started their match. I paced up and down the hall, avoiding running into people as much as possible. I never played like that unless I was joking around. My ribs hurt and I rubbed my chest, hoping the feeling would leave. I leaned against the wall and took some deep breaths. I headed back toward the Game Room but halted when I saw Zeek standing right by the entrance. He had his arms crossed and was leaning against the wall, a picture of relaxation. Instead of talking to him, I moved around him and started to step inside the Game Room.

"It's starting, you know," he said.

I stopped and turned my head to stare at him. "Yeah, that's why I'm going back in."

"Wrong. Not the game. You," he said as he pushed himself off the wall.

"Huh?"

Zeek walked closer until he was right in front of me. "You. Did you stop caring? When you killed your teammates. Did it hurt? Or did you brush it off?"

My eyes widened and I stuttered. "Of course I didn't care. It's a game."

Zeek nodded. "Yes. No turning back now. It's easier to fight, you know, when you don't care."

I looked at him like he was an alien from another planet. "Uh-huh. Okay, bye."

Zeek laughed and his voice followed me into the room. "You'll see, Ben. It's only a matter of time now."

Pearl saw me walk in and patted the spot next to her on the couch. I sat down and she informed me that our team was two matches away. We watched as our tournament bracket dwindled to the final four teams. Pearl and I started up with our team. She grinned at me and said, "We got this in the bag."

I laughed and turned towards the screen. As soon as I started focusing on the players, everything around me became a blur of nothing. I only had one goal. Defeat everyone. Win at all costs.

Pearl and I were the last ones standing again, but when I saw that the match was completed, I felt nothing. It hadn't been fun like it usually was. I gritted my teeth. We had one more round. Win at all costs.

The next two teams went and then it was our turn once more. The match was long, and eventually, it was down to two versus two, me and Pearl against two on their team. Pearl sniped one of their teammates in the head, narrowing it down to three. I was running around trying to find the last enemy when I was shot from behind. I turned, trying to save myself, but he already had the upper hand. Pearl got him while he was distracted, but my character fell down and I was out. Pearl jumped up and yelled, excited that we won.

I wasn't the last one standing. I gritted my teeth and threw my controller on the couch. Standing up, I stalked out of the room and headed home. The party would go on for another few hours but I didn't want to join. I unlocked my door and saw Zeek standing in the hall by my room, staring at me, his expression blank. I shut the door, making sure to lock it tight, and collapsed onto my chair, dropping my head to the desk. What was wrong with me?

Chapter Fourteen

FOR THE NEXT FEW days, I avoided stopping by Pearl's to hang out or even just check on her. I didn't want to talk to her. The feelings, or lack of, during the *Halo* match had been something I'd never experienced before and I didn't know how to handle it. For the first time in a while, I wished that my dad was here. My mom and I were close enough, but I had the best relationship with my dad. He always was willing to listen to me when I needed to talk and gave great advice. He never judged me or tried to tell me what to do. My mom and I were more likely to fight since I was always breaking her rules. Dumb rules, in my opinion. If my dad were here, he'd know what to do.

When the work week started again, I dragged myself there early in the morning. I'd stayed up all night rewatching all the downloaded shows on my phone and then had a hard time falling asleep. Jewel raised her eyebrows when she saw me but didn't say a word. We silently got to work trying to figure out our project.

Jewel was looking over the schematics of our project when inspiration struck me. I suddenly knew exactly how we could fit the materials we needed into the size we wanted. I grabbed a stack of paper and frantically started drawing and listing the components we needed. Jewel looked up in surprise, watching me as I worked with her mouth open. When I was finished, I handed her the papers.

"I figured it out," I said. "This is how we can make it work."

Jewel scanned the pages, her lips pursed and eyes narrowed. "Wow. You're right."

I grinned in triumph. I knew what I was doing. Jewel looked at me and her eyes narrowed even more. "This is a little advanced for you," she said.

Shrugging, I picked up the paper and made a few more notes. If it worked—and I had no doubt that it would—we would be able to use these papers and have them easily reproduced. I looked up. Jewel was still studying me with pursed lips.

"What?" I said.

"Nothing," she said. "Pearl said you haven't been by."

I lifted my shoulders and dropped them. "I've been busy."

Jewel nodded and dropped the subject. We started to gather the supplies that we had, and Jewel put in an order to Ms. Jane to get the ones we didn't have. I grinned, glee spreading through my chest. Finally, we had figured out this weapon.

***

At night the next day, I was in my room playing a mobile card game when someone knocked on my door. I opened the door and Pearl was standing there, holding a bag of chips and a plate with a few slices of pizza. When she saw me, her eyes widened and she took a step back.

"Uh. Hey," she said. "I haven't seen you in a while. I brought you pizza."

She held out the pizza and I opened my door wider to let her in. I knew I should have felt bad about not visiting her, but I couldn't bring myself to. She sat down at Tom's desk and handed me a plate with two of the four slices on it. I accepted the plate and sat down across from her.

She started talking about the party after the tournament and how there were plans for another one in two weeks. She told me how a lot of the people who joined were now regulars and were inviting other friends to join. Pearl even speculated that we'd have to expand the tournament to a two-day event at this rate. I nodded at what I thought were the right moments. It must not have been convincing, though, because Pearl scooted closer and put her hand on my arm. I stared at it; it felt foreign and weird, not like it usually did. I shrugged her hand off and her eyes widened.

"Ben," she said. "Have you—have you seen yourself lately?"

"No?" I said. "Why?"

"It's just. You're just different. You don't look well."

She motioned to my hair. "When was the last time you showered?"

I felt my hair. I hadn't even noticed. "Uh. Not that long ago," I said, lying through my teeth.

Pearl frowned, clearly not believing me. "All right. Well, I'm just going to go. You should get some rest. It looks like you aren't sleeping."

She stood up and walked out, leaving the chips and trash behind. I locked the door and went to the bathroom. The mirror wasn't kind; my eyes were hollow with dark circles dragging them down. My hair was greasy and all over the place. I honestly couldn't remember the last time I showered. My clothes had stains from days ago. I sniffed my shirt and gagged. Pearl was right. My shoulders drooped and I spent the next hour cleaning myself and my room up. Days of trash filled up two trash bags, and I even vacuumed the floor.

When I was all done, I left my room to go visit Pearl. The shower and cleaning had snapped me a little bit out of my stupor, and I knew I needed to apologize to her. Or say thank you. Or both.

I wasn't even halfway to her room when Zeek and Norman appeared next to me. I tried to step around them so I could get to Pearl's room, but they blocked me. Sighing, I stared at them both. "What do you want?" I said.

Zeek grinned. Norman said, "You need to come with us."

"Guys, I'm not using the BANEP again. I'm good," I said. I tried to sidestep them again but they continued to block me.

"Nope. Not that," said Norman. He held up a paper. I looked closer and it was titled "Transfer of Service" on the top, with Ms. Jane's signature at the bottom.

"Cool, a piece of paper," I said, trying to sidestep them again.

"This is your new assignment," said Norman. "You're going to come with us and help train soldiers. Ms. Jane approved it."

"I already have a job, thanks."

"And now instead of cleaning and working at the library, you're working for me. Wednesday, Thursday, Friday. Every week," Norman said, handing me the paper.

I stopped in my attempts to leave and took the paper. A quick scan showed me that Norman was right. Ms. Jane had assigned me to teach recruits different karate styles each day, all day. I shoved the paper back at Norman.

"It's Tuesday. And I don't teach," I said.

Norman shrugged. "That's why we're getting you today. You're going to spar with Zeek, get comfortable moving around the gym."

Zeek loomed over me, a psychotic grin on his face. "Nope," I said.

Norman shrugged again, tilting his head in a half shrug. "Your choice. But it's that or go to the prison here. You know we have one, right? Zeek's been there."

Zeek nodded. I gritted my teeth. "Fine. Let's get this over with."

They led me to the gym and Zeek stood by the door while Norman walked with me to the center of the mat. "I thought I was going to spar with Zeek?" I said.

"Me first," said Norman. "I don't know anything about fighting."

I stared at him and shrugged. Whatever. Norman paced around me while I just stood there. When he was back in front of me, he reached forward and pushed me on the shoulder. My hand shot out and grabbed his. In one smooth move, I twisted Norman around and brought my other arm up, and put him in a chokehold, tight. Norman pulled on my arm until I loosened and let go. He spun around to face me.

"You're ready," he said. Norman called for Zeek to come over, but he wasn't by the door anymore. Norman called for him again and Zeek came in from outside the gym, rubbing his stomach. Norman narrowed his eyes at him but didn't say anything.

"Start," said Norman, a creepy grin on his face.

Zeek made the first move, swinging his leg straight toward my head. I dodged, dropping to the ground and swiping my leg out, knocking him off balance. He fell to the ground, rolling until he could reach my foot. I moved it out of the way right as he reached out to grab my foot. I jumped up, standing and forming a defensive position. My body knew exactly what it was doing.

Zeek jumped up, circling me. I followed, keeping my eyes on him. I swung my fist out, aiming for his nose. He dodged by moving his head to the side, but my other fist was already there, moving faster than I knew I could move. Zeek grinned.

"This is interesting," he said. He swung his fist toward my head and I dropped down in a squat and swung my fist up to his stomach. He yelped and jumped back, a grimace on his face. Hmm, that was interesting. His stomach was already sensitive. I backed up until I was a good four feet away from him. Before he could move around me again, I rushed towards him in a bent position, aiming my shoulder for his stomach. My shoulder connected and he grunted, falling backward.

He held his hands up. "All right, I concede. This time."

I stood up straight, my expression neutral. Honestly, I didn't care what he did. I didn't care about much of anything right now. I turned toward Norman. He was watching with a malicious grin on his face.

"Perfect," he said. "You'll start tomorrow morning. We'll pick you up."

I nodded and left.

Chapter Fifteen

D URING THE NEXT FEW weeks, I saw less and less of Pearl and more and more of Norman and Zeek. Every week for three days, I taught different styles of karate to the recruits. My days ended the same: sparring with Zeek until one of us gave up. Some days I won, some days he did. Winning didn't feel like winning. It felt hollow. Everything felt hollow. It's funny. I used the machine so that I could protect Pearl, but now I didn't even bother to see her.

One day, on the way home from a particularly brutal sparring session with Zeek, I ran into Pearl. She was carrying a yoga mat. She ran up to me and hugged me.

"Ben," she said, standing on her toes. "It's been too long. Have you been avoiding me?"

I looked down into her eyes and felt nothing. No excitement, no pity, no sympathy. "No. Just been busy."

Her eyes widened. "Oh. Okay. There's another tournament next week if you want to play."

I shrugged. "Maybe."

Her eyes narrowed as she studied me. "Are you okay?"

"Never been better."

She nodded. "Right. I have good news for you. I overheard some people talking. They're picking up your sister and brother today. They'll be coming back in the afternoon."

I froze and my heart stuttered. I left Pearl standing there and went straight into my room, locking the door tight. I sat down at my desk and stared at the wall. They were coming back. For the first time in a long time, I felt something in my heart move. I thought of my siblings, out there without me, fighting to find our parents. Stumbling to the bathroom, I looked at myself in the mirror and was disgusted with what I saw. In our family, Sam was always the bright light. I was always the cloud. Now I had turned into the storm they thought I was.

I heard the lock in the door turn and I stepped out of the bathroom and stared, my heart beating like it hadn't in weeks. Tom stepped in, followed by June and my mouth dropped open. June flew to me, throwing her arms around my neck. She even had a few tears leaking out of her eyes, something that hardly ever happened. Tom had a sling over his arm and his shirt was torn and bloody.

"What happened?" I said. "What's going on?"

June stepped back, taking a good look at me. Her eyes widened and her mouth dropped open. She turned to Tom. "Sam was right."

"Right about what?" I said.

June reached out and squeezed my hand. "Don't worry. We're back now. You won't turn into a Hollow Soldier."

"Hollow Soldier?" I said.

"Yeah," said Tom. "Like in *Dark Souls*. That's what I decided to name the prisoners Norman made. Because they don't feel?"

I stared at him, my mouth hanging open. Is that what was happening to me? The door opened and Pearl walked in. "Oh good, you two are already here. We have work to do."

I stared at her and she smiled. "I'm talking about you," she said.

"But nothing is wrong with me," I said.

She reached out and pulled me into a hug. My heart stuttered again and she whispered into my ear. "Everything's going to be okay. I'm not letting you die."

***

Read on for a sneak peek of SECRET SKIES, book two of the CHIMERA SKIES series. You'll be able to see what was happening to Sam and her group while Ben was in Bunker 3.

If you enjoyed this novella, please leave a review now. They can be any length you wish and every review helps. Thank you!

Join Sharlene Healy's newsletter to keep up to date with new releases, giveaways, and more!

Chapter Sixteen

D URING THE NEXT FEW weeks, I saw less and less of Pearl and more and more of Norman and Zeek. Every week for three days, I taught different styles of karate to the recruits. My days ended the same: sparring with Zeek until one of us gave up. Some days I won, some days he did. Winning didn't feel like winning. It felt hollow. Everything felt hollow. It's funny. I used the machine so that I could protect Pearl, but now I didn't even bother to see her.

One day, on the way home from a particularly brutal sparring session with Zeek, I ran into Pearl. She was carrying a yoga mat. She ran up to me and hugged me.

"Ben," she said, standing on her toes. "It's been too long. Have you been avoiding me?"

I looked down into her eyes and felt nothing. No excitement, no pity, no sympathy. "No. Just been busy."

Her eyes widened. "Oh. Okay. There's another tournament next week if you want to play."

I shrugged. "Maybe."

Her eyes narrowed as she studied me. "Are you okay?"

"Never been better."

She nodded. "Right. I have good news for you. I overheard some people talking. They're picking up your sister and brother today. They'll be coming back in the afternoon."

I froze and my heart stuttered. I left Pearl standing there and went straight into my room, locking the door tight. I sat down at my desk and stared at the wall. They were coming back. For the first time in a long time, I felt something in my heart move. I thought of my siblings, out there without me, fighting to find our parents. Stumbling to the bathroom, I looked at myself in the mirror and was disgusted with what I saw. In our family, Sam was always the bright light. I was always the cloud. Now I had turned into the storm they thought I was.

I heard the lock in the door turn and I stepped out of the bathroom and stared, my heart beating like it hadn't in weeks. Tom stepped in, followed by June and my mouth dropped open. June flew to me, throwing her arms around my neck. She even had a few tears leaking out of her eyes, something that hardly ever happened. Tom had a sling over his arm and his shirt was torn and bloody.

"What happened?" I said. "What's going on?"

June stepped back, taking a good look at me. Her eyes widened and her mouth dropped open. She turned to Tom. "Sam was right."

"Right about what?" I said.

June reached out and squeezed my hand. "Don't worry. We're back now. You won't turn into a Hollow Soldier."

"Hollow Soldier?" I said.

"Yeah," said Tom. "Like in *Dark Souls*. That's what I decided to name the prisoners Norman made. Because they don't feel?"

I stared at him, my mouth hanging open. Is that what was happening to me? The door opened and Pearl walked in. "Oh good, you two are already here. We have work to do."

I stared at her and she smiled. "I'm talking about you," she said.

"But nothing is wrong with me," I said.

She reached out and pulled me into a hug. My heart stuttered again and she whispered into my ear. "Everything's going to be okay. I'm not lettin you die."

About Author

Sharlene Healy has been telling stories for as long as she can remember. After many twists and turns, her life road led her to her husband, who encouraged her to participate in NaNoWriMo 2013 while their son was still a baby. She now has four kids and spends most of her time juggling them as best she can. She lives on the West Coast after slowly migrating from Pennsylvania. She loves to read, craft, and generally cause mayhem.

She can be found on Facebook, Instagram, Goodreads, and TikTok. If you'd like to discuss her books, join her Facebook Group: Can't Stop Won't Stop Reading or her Discord Channel: Sharlene's Book Club.

ALSO BY

Chimera Skies

Secret Skies (Coming soon!)

9 798201 954529